For all little learner musicians, but especially for their Mothers.

And for Becky and Jo Wignell,
Rebecca Markless, Joanna Pace and
David and Megan Porter.

Library of Congress Cataloging-in-Publication Data
Porter, Sue.
Moose music/by Sue Porter.
p.   cm.
"First published in 1994 by HarperCollins UK"—T.p. verso.
Summary: No one appreciates the noise Moose makes when he plays his fiddle—until a lady moose hears him.
ISBN 0-307-17511-1: $12.95
[1. Moose—Fiction. 2. Music—Fiction. 3. Noise—Fiction.]
I. Title.
PZ7.P8339Mo 1994
[E]—dc20   93-31519   CIP   AC

First published in Great Britain by HarperCollins Publishers Ltd. in 1994.

Moose Music

Sue Porter

AN ARTISTS & WRITERS GUILD BOOK

Golden Books

Western Publishing Company, Inc.

Moose was walking in the woods when he came across a mud puddle. There, sticking out of the mud, was an old fiddle.

"Fantastic!" Moose said and he pounced on it. He drew the bow across the rusty strings. This made a dreadful ear-splitting screech that rattled all the leaves on all the trees for miles around.

"Lovely," said Moose.

Down river, the beavers were building a dam.
"Come on, everyone," called Father Beaver,
"one last big effort. **HEAVE!**"

sCRRREEEECHH! went the fiddle.

CRRAAASHH! went the dam.
"Get that moose away from here!"
yelled Father Beaver.

But Moose had already gone.

Bear was busy stealing honey. He stretched out his paw as far as he could toward the nest.

*sCRRE*E*ECHH!* went the fiddle.

CRRAAASHH! went Bear.
"Take that horrible instrument
elsewhere!" he shouted.

Moose didn't wait to be told twice.

Jack was cutting down trees. They always
fell just where he wanted them to.

*sCRR**EEE**CHH!* went the fiddle.

CRRAAASHH! went the tree.
"Come back here!" shouted Jack.

But Moose thought he'd better not.

Moose sat on a log and hung his head.
"It seems that no one around here
appreciates good music," he said. And he
got up and plodded sadly off into the forest.

At last he came to a beautiful and deserted place. He watched the sun slowly sinking behind the mountains. Lifting his fiddle, he began to play with all his heart.

"What lovely music,"
said a voice from the trees.

"It makes me feel like singing,"
said the lady moose.
"Please do," said Moose.

The grating of her voice was every bit as horrible as Moose's fiddle. It rasped and howled and echoed around the lakes and mountains.

Moose gasped. His ears shook. His eyes bulged. He quivered all over. It was just the sort of sound that mooses really like.

Moose was in love.

"Lovely," said Moose. "Let's do it again."
"Yes," said the lady moose. "Let's make
moose music together."